Avocado
Baby

Persea gratissima

AVOCADO BABY
A RED FOX BOOK 978 1 862 30685 1

First published in Great Britain by Jonathan Cape,
an imprint of Random House Children's Books
A Random House Group Company

Jonathan Cape edition published 1982
Red Fox edition published 1994
This Red Fox edition published 2008

1 3 5 7 9 10 8 6 4 2

Red Fox books are published by Random House Children's Books,
61–63 Uxbridge Road, London W5 5SA

www.kidsatrandomhouse.co.uk
www.rbooks.co.uk

Addresses for companies within The Random House Group Limited can
be found at: www.randomhouse.co.uk/offices.htm

THE RANDOM HOUSE GROUP Limited Reg. No. 954009

A CIP catalogue record for this book is available from the British Library.

Printed in China

This edition is part of a box set and cannot be sold or returned separately.

Avocado
Baby

John Burningham

RED FOX

For Emms

Mr and Mrs Hargraves and their two children were not very strong. Mrs Hargraves was expecting another baby, and they all hoped it would not be as weak as they were.

The new baby was born and all the family were very pleased. Mr and Mrs Hargraves brought the baby home and it grew but, as they feared, it did not grow strong. Mrs Hargraves found feeding the baby difficult. It did not like food or want to eat much.

"Whatever can I do," wailed Mrs Hargraves.
"The baby doesn't like eating anything I make
and it looks so weak."
"Why don't you give it that avocado pear?"
said the children.

In the fruit bowl on the table there was
an avocado pear. Nobody knew how it had
got there because the Hargraves never
bought avocados. Mrs Hargraves cut the
pear in half, mashed it and gave it to
the baby, who ate it all up.
From that day on an amazing thing
happened. The baby became very strong.

It was getting so strong it could

break out from
the straps on its
high chair,

pull other children uphill in a cart

wrench off the side of its cot.
And each day Mrs Hargraves gave
the baby avocado pear.

One night a burglar got into the house.

The baby woke up and heard the burglar
moving about downstairs.
The baby picked up a broom,

and chased the burglar. The burglar was so
frightened at being chased by a baby that he
dropped his bag and ran out of the house.

The next day Mr Hargraves put a notice
on the gate. "That should keep the
burglars away," he said.

The baby would help carry the shopping, move the furniture and push the car when it would not start.

One day two bullies were waiting for
the children in the park.

The bullies started being very nasty to the children. The baby did not like that and jumped out of its push-chair,

picked up the bullies and

threw them into the pond.

The baby gets stronger every day and of course it is still eating avocado pears.

Persea gratissima